THE PERFECT ROMANCE

Getting Every Need Met

Jeanie Traub ND, NHC

"All Bible verses were taken from the Amplified Bible app."

The Amplified Bible (AMP) is an English translation of the Bible produced jointly by The Zondervan Corporation and The Lockman Foundation. The first edition was published in 1965. It is largely a revision of the American Standard Version of 1901, with reference made to various texts in the original languages. It is designed to "amplify" the text by using a system of punctuation and other typographical features to bring out all shades of meaning present in the original text.

Dedication

This book is dedicated to my precious grandchildren and to those who desire a more fulfilling life here on earth. My deepest desire is to help you become all that you were created to be. To understand how special, how gifted, and how amazing each of you are! It is to help you become who you were created to be and to discover a passionate love that everyone desires.

Acknowledgment

To all my friends and family that have been supportive of my journey here on earth. From living in the ways of the world to finding a much higher way to live, from deaths door to living a supernatural life, I cannot thank you enough. Life does not always go the way we want, but life can be restored to better than before.

A special thanks to my amazing husband Greg, who married me while I was still walking through major health challenges. You gave me the love and support to keep going on and achieving my health goals. Plus, you are a lot of fun! We sure enjoy life together!

Contents

1

My Story

Hi, my name is Jeanie Traub. I have an amazing man in my life who meets all my needs. It is incredibly awesome how he knows every little detail about me.

Sometimes I feel like I'm walking in heaven on earth because of how loving, gentle, and kind he is. It wasn't always this way in my life, but now I have found my true love. I wanted to write about him to help you find your true love.

It took me a while to find my perfect love in life. I must admit that it took a few marriages. But after I found my love, it all seemed worth the ups and downs that my life had taken.

I didn't always have an easy life. Life can give us some hurts, disappointments, and pain. But looking back, now I can see how I was being prepared for my one true love.

I can't wait to share so much more.

• Looking Back at Life•

As a little girl, I think we all anxiously await our knight in shining armor. You know, the one who will whisk us away and protect us from all harm. Someone who loves us just for being ourselves. We try to look our best, smell our best, and be our best, right? Someone who will cherish us for just being us, who understands our ways and always compliments us! Well, I found him, so just wait!

There were pivotal moments in my life while growing up that helped me shape myself and my beliefs. Some of them were good, and some probably not so good. I had my moment with rebellion but didn't care much for that route. I preferred being good.

My dream was to get married, have a little boy and a little girl, and live happily ever after. You know, like the television shows we grew up with. Well, that kind of happened, but not totally. After ten years and having my little girl and my little boy, my marriage ended in divorce, like fifty percent of marriages do.

I was ready to tackle the world, me and my two children. I didn't know enough about life yet to know how cruel some people could be.

I lost my mom to a short battle with cancer. That really changed my life. It's interesting how losing someone who is such a part of your life can change everything.

I was living in a city in a different state and truly felt all alone, except for my two young children, of course. They were my life. Their father had moved out of state not long after our divorce, so he wasn't around. It was just me and my children against the world. I could look into their beautiful eyes, and it would keep me going forever. Children are so precious.

• **More Hope for a Brighter Future**•

Well, eventually, I met another man who became my next husband. I would melt when I looked into his eyes. I felt like the happiest woman in the world. We were good together. We had a lot of the same likes and dislikes and enjoyed many of the same things. Life was finally good . . . for a while. Without getting into a lot of details, it ended after seven years. I was devastated! Did you know that sixty percent of second marriages fail? How tragic!

Well, I knew how to survive. I had done it before. So, back into the world we went, me and my two children, healing from the wounds of disappointments and hurts.

Women are resilient, right? I was blessed to have a great job to help raise my children. The hardest part for me was not being able to be there for them more. Any single parent realizes that all the responsibility is on them. I looked at it as an honor to have them in my life.

There were a few challenging moments in their teen years, but overall, we tried to enjoy each day.

2

Being A Single Parent

I was in a church and involved as much as I had time. God was a big part of my life. I grew up in church and knew God loved me. We went on Sundays and had an occasional Bible study here and there, like most churchgoers. A good sermon always sets me off to a good start for the week.

I knew my assignment in life was to raise my children the best I knew how. I think every parent does that, but some are much better at it than others. We all do the best we can in life.

There is always someone who will do things better, but there are also those who do a lot worse. I learned a lot about parenting. It's on-the-job training, and there is no such thing as a perfect parent or a perfect child. Raising children is a challenge, but the rewards are great.

• Going Deeper•

My children are now raised and out of the house, quite an accomplishment that some parents have a hard time with. I could see their enthusiasm, the same enthusiasm I once had . . . world, here I come! Oh, how I wished I could protect them from the ups and downs of life. I had equipped them the best I knew how.

I was still holding onto the hope that maybe one day I would meet the real mister right, but I was pretty guarded at this point. My health wasn't quite where it should be, despite my workouts and constantly watching what I ate.

As a few years passed, I had been diagnosed with a few things. Nothing I couldn't work through, but I did want the best lifestyle that I could have. You know, go to work, work out a few times a week, eat lean, have fun with friends, and go to church. But for some reason, it wasn't right. My health kept getting worse and I was getting more and more depleted. The next few years were spent struggling at work and trying to find out what was going on with my physical health.

Doctor's visits were not my favorite thing, but I found myself there quite often. I was on heart medications, had iron transfusions and underwent numerous tests for neurological problems, which were eventually diagnosed as seizures. I was always optimistic that these things would change with time.

Well, they did, but for the worst. In May of 2000, I was diagnosed with terminal cancer and given a few months to live. I was so sick and depleted from fatigue and having numerous seizures that I was just hopeful for a few hours to feel good.

Where was my knight in shining armor? Would I ever have my dreams fulfilled, or was my life over?

With only five minutes to function before I had a seizure, I prayed. My prayer was, if it was my time, then take me home. But if not, bring into my life the things I need for a total and complete healing.

3

My Knight in Shining Armor

As I lay in my bed listening to Christian music, my Savior arrived! He was alive, real, and tangible. He touched my heart in such a tender way and told me everything was going to be alright. I fell in love. He didn't want anything from me but to just love Him back.

There weren't enough hours in the day to spend with my best friend, Jesus. He made me glow with happiness and gave me hope for a much brighter future. He loved me just the way I was: broken and dying.

I felt His presence with me all the time and He never let me go. We spent time talking to each other, holding each other's hearts, and gazing into each other's eyes.

A love I had never felt before. He told me to rise above my circumstances and trust in Him only. Medical science had no answers for me. All the money in the world could not have saved or healed me. But Jesus . . . He did! He guided my steps, held my hand, encouraged me, gave me strength, and was always there for me.

Wow! My true love came to me. He wrapped His loving arms around me and guided me back to health.

He taught me to walk in His ways and not the world's ways. He taught me His way of thinking and His way of doing things. Not my will but Yours, Lord. I learned to lay down all the knowledge of the world I had learned and to learn His ways . . . a new way. A supernatural way to live in heaven on earth.

Isaiah 55:8-9 says, *"For My thoughts are not your thoughts, neither are your ways My ways," says the Lord.*

"For as the heavens are higher than the earth, so are My ways higher than your ways and My thoughts than your thoughts."

He gave me visions and dreams to strengthen my spirit and learn how to love myself and this crazy world. He showed me how people are wounded and hurting and how He desired for them to know Him. To have such an intimate walk with Him that they would know His heart.

To listen to His wise counsel and not rely on their own knowledge. But to learn His wisdom and knowledge. And all I had to do was ask, "How do You want me to see this, Lord?" Then listen to His kind reply. Then I could find total peace or have it my way. Free will is really rejecting His higher ways.

How my love journey continued forever. I continue to learn and grow in His ways. Walking through life with the lover of my heart and soul. He completes me! And He healed me! What a tremendous love story of living in the possibility of such a deeper love. How complete I am. How much more I have to give to those He brings into my life. Continually filling me with His love to give to others.

4

Walking in the Supernatural

I don't know where you are in life, but I can give you this advice: no matter what you think is best, it may not be the best for you. You cannot outthink the wisdom of God. He created the universe and you. He loves you more than you can imagine, and He longs for you to get to know Him on a personal basis – not intellectually, but through a real, tangible, and extraordinary relationship.

He delights in you. He loves to see you smile, and He loves to give you gifts. It's a phenomenal journey, with your personal spiritual guide to help you through life, to look out for you, and to guide you into your true purpose here on earth.

You are unique, and His instructions for you are unique. He can tell you and teach you things that will help you along your journey. Do you know that you have spiritual gifts that were put inside of you – things that make you feel fulfilled and complete? And each one of us is different, with different gifts. When we walk with Jesus, we find out so many things that we would never find out on our own.

This life is one gift He gave you. How you steward this life and the gifts He has given you is your gift back to Him. He will help you walk in a supernatural way with Him. You see, people are not perfect, but He is. The things people, sometimes church people, have done to you are not God. The things that have happened that man has done are not a reflection of who God is.

I meet injured people all the time who someone has hurt or said something that hurt them in some way, and they blame God. But God will heal their body, mind, emotions, and hearts if people let Him.

Are you looking for the true love of your life? He's right here with you now. He's been waiting for you to desire Him to be in your life, to let Him into your heart completely and fully. Then your life can be restored, healed of all the hurts that life has given you. He will hold your hand and help you rise above it all – above the world's ways and into His heavenly ways. Then you will start to walk in heaven on earth.

You will walk with Jesus every day, and He will guide you into a supernatural life.

5

You are Supernatural

Did you know that you are a spirit living in a body, and you can invite the Spirit of the living God to live in you too? You were made, created, or let's say "wired" for a particular purpose to accomplish while you are here living on earth. Asking God into your life will enable you to live as He had planned before you were born.

There are millions of good stories out there and millions of bad stories. There are millions who have overcome horrific things in life. But I want to talk about you. What purpose does God have for you, and how can you achieve your purpose?

Here's a hint . . . it's usually the thing that brings great emotion to you when the subject is brought up. Something that moves you when you talk about it. It's something that interests you, and you feel a great passion for it. It's usually something that you love to learn about or talk about. You were wired and created for that purpose. It's what you should be doing in life.

I've heard of so many parents putting an expectation on

their children to do something they thought they should be doing. Worse yet, they only approve of them if they follow the dreams of their parents. The child, as an adult, finally comes to that realization and makes great changes to follow his or her own dream. It is something inside of you that lines up with what you were created to do. It brings you fulfillment and pleasure, joy in life, happiness inside, and a reason to wake up each day and give back to the world and do what you were created to do!

• Unleashing your Potential•

Unleashing your potential is like reading the blueprint of your life. When you look back, you can see how different key events in your life contributed to discovering who you were meant to be.

The various experiences, whether good or bad, will give you a passion or cause that is significant to you. Many are born with an obvious gift, such as a great singer or someone who loves to be in front of others, reporting daily events. But for most of us, it's a bit more complex. We have to put together a more complex matrix to figure out the best passion from our life experiences. I'll explain mine as we go along to give you a grid for your life.

•The Past•

I can remember when I was about four years old, asking my mom what happened to people when they were really hurt or sick. She explained it to me. Later in life, she became very sick and was hospitalized. Within a few weeks, she was gone. She had died of cancer.

How could that happen? She had been healthy up until that time. How could cancer take her life and take her away from our family? It was one of those "bad events" that eventually turned around in my own life.

At the time, my mind went to questions like "how did she get sick?" "What caused this?" and "How can I help heal it?" Two of my cousins became oncology nurses to help those suffering from cancer. But I was wired differently.

Years went by, and I always loved to "help others". So, in every job I had, I turned it into an opportunity to help people. For instance, I sold real estate, but to me, I was helping people to get into their dream homes. The same thing happened when I was a mortgage loan officer. I wanted people to have as great of an experience as possible and enjoy the process of achieving their dream. My gift was helping others in a more caring, personal way.

●Bad Story Turned to Good●

Twenty-one years after I lost my mom to cancer, I was diagnosed with terminal cancer. I was given three to six months to live. It was a rare cancer called leiomyosarcoma. You can read my story in "The Healing Gift – Defeating Cancer" if you would like to know more. But for now, I want to stay on the subject of what "you" are created for and help you get there.

Well, my opportunity, or really my "crash course" on what causes cancer and how to get rid of it, became my own reality. After many days of gathering information on alternative ways of dealing with cancer, reality hit. I was down to only a few months to live. I was having numerous seizures, memory loss, and basically dying.

I gave up trying to learn about cancer and threw everything away. I knew at this point it was impossible for me to figure this out on my own. I prayed, "God, bring the things into my life for a total and complete healing," having faith that He would. I learned what caused cancer and how to get rid of it.

It was an amazing journey of learning a new way of life. I then applied what I had learned, had a teachable spirit, and my passion was fulfilled! I now have taught hundreds of others how to get rid of cancer in their life. I was an overcomer and found what I was created to do. With passion, I continue to help those who will listen and learn this amazing gift of how to take care of your body.

I want to give you hope that each experience you have in life will lead you to a greater potential in you. Each job, each relationship can keep leading you to your life's purpose. Tapping into the spirit in you will help balance your life tremendously.

The way you have to feed your body good nutritional foods is also the way you have to feed your mind and spirit. I greatly encourage you not to neglect your spiritual relationship with God. It is where you will find what you were truly created for. The gifts that were given to you when you were born.

6

Enjoy the Journey

As I was growing up, I always felt there was more to life. The world's ways sometimes seemed, honestly, kind of silly. Go to school, get a job, raise a family, enjoy your grandchildren . . . then die. Buy stuff, compare your life to others, and always feel like you should be doing more. Some people feel like they have to keep up with everyone else around them . . . or please their parents.

Well, here's the news flash! You are unique and made for a purpose here on earth. A higher purpose than you can imagine!

•Child of a King•

Everyone here on earth has a Father in heaven who is all wisdom, all-knowledge, all-knowing, and knows everything about them. Yes, He created you! He loves you, has been watching you grow up, and is waiting with great expectation for you to get to know Him.

He is loving, kind, supportive, forgiving, and will guide you into who you were created to be: an amazing child of a King!

And Father God has a son, Jesus, who will be your best friend through eternity – both here on earth and in heaven. Jesus is our gift, our best friend, our Savior, and our deliverer!

He died on the cross for your sins! If you had been the only person on earth, He would have died just for you! He redeemed mankind from the curses in this world to live a better life "in Christ."

No one else is responsible for our life or our spirituality. We can choose to be Spirit-led believers and develop our spirituality through Christ. It means we have a closer walk with the Lord and have chosen His ways over our own. To live this way, we need His power living on the inside of us.

Matthew 6:33 teaches us, "But seek (aim and strive after) first of all His kingdom and His righteousness (His way of doing and being right), and then all things taken together will be given you besides".

Wow! And His will is always good and perfect (James

1:17), and when we surrender our will and ask Him to guide us, He will! And as we pursue Him, He will continue to show us great and mighty things we did not know (Jeremiah 33:3). And everyone has their unique destiny if they choose it. The Holy Spirit is here on earth to be our guide, our mentor, and lead us into a godly life that can only be achieved with His help.

The Father, Son, and Holy Spirit are the three Gods in one, each having their unique functions to help us have a better life . . . and they run the entire universe!

Then why the evil . . .

•Satan: The Father of Lies•

Why do bad things happen if there's a God? All of us ask this question . . . and many turn away from God when bad things happen. They think that God did them.

It saddens God when we blame Him for the bad things that happen. He gave man much more power than most believe, and He gave us free will – to either follow Him and listen to Him or to do things our own way.

Then there is pure evil. This was a lesson I had to learn. Evil people do evil things. The wolf in sheep's clothing has become progressively worse in our world. Deception is Satan's weapon against God's people.

This one I hesitated writing, but here it goes . . .

"Man's knowledge is stupidity to God."

"For this world's wisdom is foolishness (absurdity and stupidity) with God, for it is written, He lays hold of the wise in their [own] craftiness; [Job 5:13.]
1 Corinthians 3:19

Ouch!

We have a world full of doctorates, PhDs, master's degrees, etc., but our world is still a mess! That does not mean these degrees are worthless, but they pale in comparison to the wisdom of God.

34

If everyone here on earth lined up with God and their assignment and purpose, we would have a better world!

Unfortunately, we haven't done that. Many times we think we know more than God … a huge mistake! And Satan is a master manipulator at perpetuating lies.

If we knew the truth of how evil some people can be, we would guard our hearts and lives much better.

7

The Bible

The Bible is God speaking to us, helping us to live a better life. It is full of stories about how God intervened in people's lives. He worked through everyday people like you and me to make huge changes in the world. Imagine how amazing our world would be if we all loved Jesus with all our hearts, soul, and mind, and followed Him to become who He created us to be.

He's calling you!

●Separation●

God wants the church to unite and be a powerful force here on earth. We don't accomplish that with a good idea . . . but we can with a God idea.

There is evil on earth but the light of God can push it back, convert some, and overtake evil. Believe me, Satan is doing his part in converting God's people to do evil. We, people, need to do our part. Then unite, network together, and fulfill the Great Commission.

●The Great Commission●

"Go then and make disciples of all the nations, baptizing *them into the Father and of the Son and of the Holy Spirit,*

Teaching them to observe everything that I have commanded you, and behold, I am with you all the days (perpetually, uniformly, and on every occasion), to the [very] close and consummation of the age. Amen (so let it be)."

Matthew 28: 19,20 Amplified Bible

Yes, God wants you!

We need all people, all genders, all ages, everywhere, to be disciples of Jesus Christ.

If you have never said the sinner's prayer, let me lead you now. It is one of the most important decisions in this life that you will ever make . . . and the best decision you will make.

Dear Heavenly Father,

I come before You today and ask that You wash away all of my sins. I ask for Jesus to come into my heart and for You to fill me with your Holy Spirit to walk a new way here on earth, a new supernatural way. I lay down my will and ask for Your will to be done in my life from this day forward.

I ask that You teach me, train me, and raise me up to be who you created me to be . . . a disciple and ambassador of Jesus Christ. Help me to fulfill my divine destiny. I choose to follow You from this day forward.

Give me wisdom beyond my years and help me to make this world a better place. In Jesus' name, Amen.

•Books in Heaven•

Before you were born, Father God, Jesus, and Holy Spirit wrote a book about your perfect life in Christ . . . your destiny (see Ps. 139:16). This is how they saw you living life triumphantly and what you were created for, your unique blueprint to life: a life of miracles, freedom, and living heaven on earth.

WOW!

We can be guided by the Holy Spirit and do what He tells us to do. It is uniting with the spirit of God and not walking in our own flesh or our own ways.

When we do this, we can reach the hearts of people in such a powerful way that we could never do on our own.

•Getting Prepared•

All of us have been wounded by life in one way or another: betrayals, hurts, disappointments, tragedies, and traumas. These wounds can keep us from God's best in our lives.

So let's get started with getting ourselves healed and move forward in a much better state of being.

Heavenly Father,

I ask that You remove all hindrances from me that are preventing me from being the best that I can be. I ask that

You take all my disappointments, traumas, betrayals I have felt, lies I have believed, and any other unjust things that have happened in my life away from me today. I lay this all at the cross today and give this to You.

Thank You, Jesus, for Your sacrifice, so I could live my life in a better way starting today. Free from the world's ways and fully embracing and living life Your way. Help me to live in heaven on earth from this day forward by uniting with You as a powerful force here on earth. Guide me, protect me from all evil, and give me the gift of discernment to see the deception in people and in this world. Give me the wisdom to guard my heart and guide me each and every day. In Jesus' name, Amen.

8

Walking in the Kingdom of God

We can learn from people who have been walking in God's Kingdom and get inspired by them for our new walk. Some of my mentors have been:

- Patricia King
- Kevin Zadai
- Jesse Duplantis

There are many more that you may be led to learn from. Be led by the Holy Spirit. If you don't get a good feeling about the message, run! Unfortunately, not all churches teach living a supernatural life in Christ.

There are also amazing television programs to help you learn more about God's ways.

- It's Supernatural with Sid Roth
- CBN with Gordon Robertson
- Daystar with Joni Lamb

These people and programs will inspire you and strengthen your new walk.

Learn all you can, apply it to your life, and become all
God has created you to be!

You are a miracle!

Love and Blessings!

Jeanie, a child of God

You can read my next book, "My Walk-Through Heaven".

 To learn more, visit my website:

www.jeanietraubministries.com

Spread the love. If this book has touched your heart, help me spread the love of Jesus. Purchase five books and give them to your friends and family that need a touch from God!

About the author

Jeanie Traub is an internationally known Natural Health Consultant, Naturopathic Doctor, speaker, author, and ordained minister. She has dedicated her studies to specializing in orthomolecular medicine and nutrition to help her clients achieve better health. Jeanie has ministered health and healing to many through their battle with cancer. She has been featured on Christian television and radio shows.